Johnny Lion's Book

Johnny Lion's Book

by Edith Thacher Hurd
Pictures by Clement Hurd

HarperCollins*Publishers*

Library of Congress Cataloging-in-Publication Data
Hurd, Edith Thacher.
    Johnny Lion's book / by Edith Thacher Hurd ; pictures by Clement Hurd.
        p.   cm. — (An I can read book)
    Summary: When his parents go out hunting, Johnny Lion stays home and experiences
exciting adventures reading a book about a baby lion who goes out into the world and
gets lost.
    ISBN 0-06-029334-9 (lib. bdg.) — ISBN 0-06-444297-7 (pbk.)
    [1. Lions—Fiction.   2. Animals—Infancy—Fiction.   3. Books and reading—Fiction.]
I. Hurd, Clement, ill.   II. Title.   III. Series.
PZ7.H956 Jp   2001   00-32027
[E]—dc21

2   3   4   5   6   7   8   9   10
❖
New Harper Trophy Edition, 2001

To Susan

One day Mother Lion

said to Father Lion,

"Johnny can read."

"Oh, really?" said Father Lion.

"Yes, really," said Mother Lion.

9

"I am going out to buy him
a new book,"
said Mother Lion.

Mother Lion went out to buy Johnny

a new book.

She looked and looked.

At last she found a book

about a baby lion.

The book was called

The Little Lion.

Mother Lion took the book home
to Johnny.

Johnny was very happy to have a boo
that he could read all by himself
when his mother and father
went out hunting.

"Be a good little lion,"

said Mother Lion.

"Do not go out of the house."

"Oh, no," said Johnny Lion.

"I will not go out of the house.

I will read my book all day long."

13

"Good-bye," said Mother Lion.

"Good-bye," said Father Lion.

"We will bring you something good to eat."

14

Mother and Father Lion went away.

Johnny Lion sat down to read.

At first he did not read very well.

He tried and tried,

until he could read the story.

Once there was
a mother lion
and
a father lion
and a baby lion.

"Just like me," said Johnny Lion.

"Only I am not a baby."

The baby lion's name was

Oscar P. Lion.

"Oh," said Johnny.

"What a nice name for a baby."

One day
Oscar P. Lion's
mother and father
went out hunting.
The baby lion
stayed at home to play

"Oh," said Johnny Lion,

"just like me.

But I am too old to play.

I stay at home to read."

Johnny Lion turned the page.

He read.

Oscar P. Lion sat down.

He tried to think of

something to do.

He tried to think of

something to play.

But he could not.

Then little Oscar P. Lion

said to himself,

"I am tired of staying at home

all by myself.

I will go out into the world."

So Oscar P. Lion

walked out of his house.

He walked right into the world.

The yellow sun smiled

on the little lion.

The tall grass tickled him.

A happy bird sang to him.

Little Oscar P. Lion was happy too

He smelled a big red flower.

"Oh, what a nice world,"

said Oscar P. Lion.

"But I am very hungry.
I will go hunting just like
my mother and father."

Little Oscar P. Lion did not
know how to hunt very well.

He climbed a big tree.

Lots of good things to eat

ran under the tree.

But little Oscar P. Lion

was afraid to jump down

and eat them.

So at last little Oscar P. Lion

had to climb down out of the tree.

He saw lots of good things to eat.

He ran after them.

He ran and ran.

But he could not catch any of them.

Then Oscar P. Lion lay very still.

He lay still in the tall, tall grass.

But he could not catch anything good to eat.

Not even a bug.

Poor little Oscar P. Lion.

He was too small to catch anything

He was very tired.

He was very hot.

He was very, very hungry.

Oscar P. Lion came to a cool, dark river.

"Oh," said Oscar P. Lion, "what a nice river.

I am so hot.

I will go swimming."

Oscar P. Lion swam and swam.
But he was so little that he did
not know very much about rivers.

He did not know that something
was looking at him.

"This is fun," said Oscar P. Lion.

"This is much more fun
than playing at home."

All this time
something lay still and quiet,
looking at Oscar P. Lion.

The something had two little eyes.

The something had big white teeth.

The something had a long tail.

The tail went

swish—swish—swish

the dark, cool river.

Little Oscar swam
closer and closer to the something
with two eyes,
the big white teeth,
and the long tail going
swish—swish—swish
in the cool, dark river.

Suddenly little Oscar P. Lion
saw the two eyes,
the white teeth,
and the tail swishing.

He swam to shore.

JUST IN TIME.

Then the little lion ran.

He ran and ran.

He was so scared that

he could not stop running.

At last he came to a place

he did not know.

He had never been there before.

He was lost.

"Oh, oh," said little Oscar P. Lion.

"I am lost."

Just then Oscar P. Lion

heard a noise.

He tried to hide.

But there were no rocks or trees.

Oscar P. Lion put his

paws over his eyes.

The noise came closer and closer.

"Why, Oscar P. Lion!" said somebody.

"What are you doing here?"

The little lion opened his eyes.

There were his very own

mother and father.

They were so glad

to see their little lion

that they both gave him a big hug.

But then Mother Lion said,

"What you did was bad.

You did not stay at home and play.

You will have to go to bed

without any supper."

"Oh," said Father Lion,

"I have been out hunting all day long.

have a big steak for my little lion.

Couldn't he go to bed

ight AFTER supper?"

"Well, just this time,"

aid Mother Lion.

So Oscar P. Lion went home

and ate a great BIG steak.

But he had to go to bed

RIGHT after supper.

Johnny Lion stopped reading.

He closed the book.

Just then his mother and father

came home from hunting.

"What did you do all day?"

said Father Lion.

"I went out into the world,"

said Johnny Lion.

"Oh, no!" said Mother Lion.

"I went hunting," Johnny said.

"Come, come," said Father Lion.

"I got chased," said Johnny Lion.

"Johnny!" Mother said.

"I got lost," Johnny said.

"What, what, what?" Father Lion said.

"But somebody found me."

"WHO?" said Mother and Father Lion.

"YOU!" Johnny Lion laughed.

"I was only fooling.

That's what happened in my book

"Really?" Mother Lion said.

"Truly?" Father Lion said.

"Really, truly," Johnny Lion said.

"I stayed at home all day

and read my book."

"I thought so all the time,"

said Mother Lion.

Then Mother and Father Lion

gave Johnny Lion a great big hug.

"But," said Johnny Lion,

"now I am very hungry."

"Have a steak," said Father Lion.

"Do I have to go to bed
RIGHT after supper?" Johnny said.

"But why?" said Mother Lion.

"Oscar had to," Johnny said.

"But you know what Oscar did,"
said Mother Lion.

"He had a lot of fun,"
said Johnny Lion.

"But I wouldn't want to
go to bed RIGHT AFTER supper."

And he didn't!

He ate his great big steak.

And then he stayed up

very, very late.

He stayed up until

he almost fell asleep.

hen Mother Lion tucked him into bed.

'm glad I'm Johnny Lion,"

hnny said.

And not Oscar P.?" Father Lion said.

'es," said Johnny sleepily.

o are we,"

id Mother and Father Lion.

Then they kissed

their little lion good night.

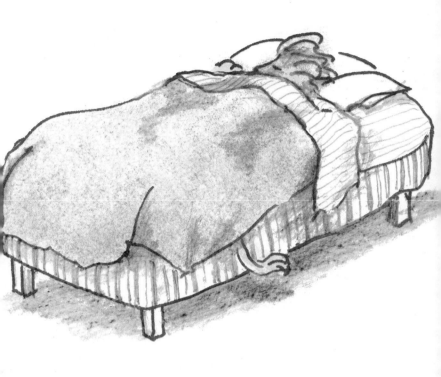

But Johnny Lion

was already fast asleep.

The End